How th
Cracke

retold by Alison Adams
illustrated by Bill Greenhead

"Hi, Turtle," said Crocodile.
"Do you want to play in the mud with me today?"

"No, Crocodile," said Turtle. "Look at my shell. It's so shiny! I want to keep my shell looking like new."

"Your shell does look good,"
said Crocodile.

"I know," said Turtle. "I try to
take care of it. I don't want to start
looking like you."

6

"Turtle! What is wrong with the way I look? Why do you say such mean things?" asked Crocodile.

Parrot and Monkey were playing high up in the tree. "Who said something mean, Crocodile?" shouted Monkey.

"Turtle did," said Crocodile.

"You do that all the time, Turtle. You should be careful about what you say," said Monkey.

"Let's just talk about something different," said Crocodile.

"Parrot, your feathers look great today," said Crocodile.

"Thanks! Some birds are having a party and I want to look my best," said Parrot.

"Can I go to the party, Parrot?" asked Turtle.

"You can, but I'm not strong enough to carry you," said Parrot.

"Why not?" asked Turtle. "You know, your feathers don't look so great."

"Turtle, you are mean!" said Parrot.

Jaguar and Buzzard came along. "Buzzard, can you take me to the party?" asked Turtle. "You're strong enough to carry me there."

"All right. I'll try," said Buzzard. "I'd like to help you, Turtle."

So Buzzard carried Turtle way up high off the ground.

"Now, don't say anything, Turtle. You will fall if you open your mouth. I will tell you some stories," said Buzzard. And Buzzard talked and talked.

"Buzzard," said Turtle, not thinking, "you talk too much." Then Turtle fell all the way down to the ground. Thump! Crocodile and Parrot and Monkey and Jaguar ran over to see if Turtle was all right.

"Turtle!" said Crocodile. "Now your shell has cracks in it!"

"Oh no!" said Turtle.

"Don't worry. We think your shell looks better than before!" said Crocodile and Parrot and Monkey and Jaguar.

"You are very good to me," said Turtle.

"And now," said Jaguar, "when we look at your shell, we'll know—"

"To think before we talk!" they all said together.